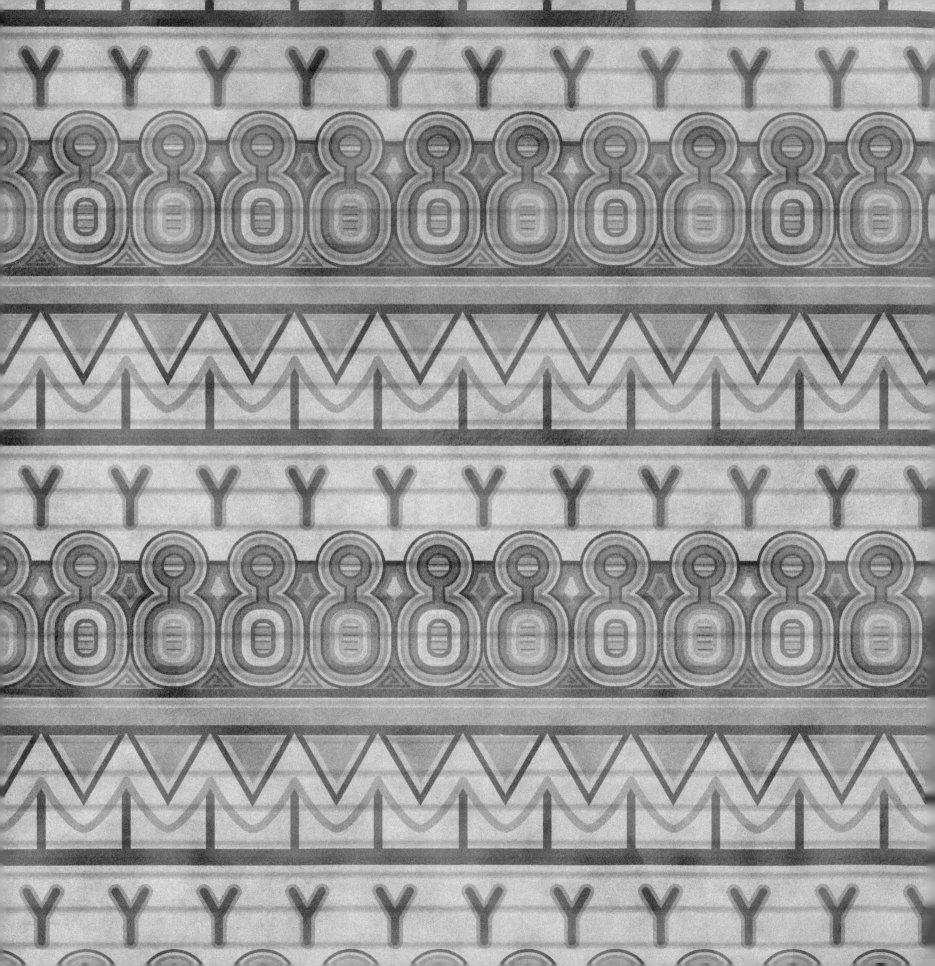

Licensed exclusively to Top That Publishing Ltd
Tide Mill Way, Woodbridge, Suffolk, IP12 1AP, UK
www.topthatpublishing.com
Copyright © 2014 Tide Mill Media
All rights reserved
0 2 4 6 8 9 7 5 3 1
Manufactured in China

Illustrated by Barbara Cantini
Retold by Susie Linn

ISBN 978-1-78445-253-7

A catalogue record for this book is available from the British Library

Anansi
the Clever Spider

Illustrated by
Barbara Cantini

Retold by
Susie Linn

Anansi the spider looked at the world around him and sighed a big sigh. He was a very clever, very wise spider – and he knew a lot about most things. But he wanted to be cleverer and wiser still!

'It'll be easy!' said Anansi to nobody in particular.
'I'll simply gather up all the wonderful knowledge
in the world ... all the brilliant cleverness ... and
all the super skills to do everything!'

First, Anansi had a big problem to solve.

'Where am I going to keep all the wisdom and cleverness when I find it?' he thought to himself. 'I'll need something VERY big and VERY safe to put it in!'

So Anansi set to work and made an
ENORMOUS pot especially for the
task. In fact, it was SO enormous
that Anansi had trouble lifting it!

'Herrumph! Gerrumph! Grooaaan!'
he muttered under his breath.

The next day, Anansi set out with his pot in search of every bit of wisdom that he could find. He travelled far and wide and saw lots of wonderful new things. But most importantly, he learnt lots, too!

Every day, Anansi added new things to his big pot of wisdom – and every day his pot became heavier!

Finally, there was no space in the pot for anything else. Which was just as well, because Anansi could hardly lift it!

Then Anansi started to worry.

'Where can I hide my pot of wisdom to keep it safe?' he thought, looking around and scratching his head with one of his eight legs.

'Will it be safe in a hole in the ground?' he wondered. 'No, the rabbits live there.'

'Maybe it'll be safe in a cave.' he pondered. 'No, the bats live there.'

'Or in the forest?' he considered. 'No ... all kinds of chattering creatures live there!'

Just as Anansi was running out of ideas, he spotted a thorn tree standing all on its own. Its trunk was covered in huge spikes – and even its leaves were spiky!

'Perfect!' shouted Anansi in delight.

Using vines to tie his enormous pot
to his tummy, Anansi started to climb
the tree ... very slowly!

Anansi was so busy struggling with his heavy pot that he didn't notice his son, Ntikuma, watching his every move.

'What a meal he's making of it!' laughed Ntikuma to himself. And he was right! Every time Anansi tried to climb the spiky tree, the pot of wisdom slipped and slid, making climbing very difficult indeed.

At last, Ntikuma could keep quiet no longer.

'Hey, Dad!' he shouted. 'Tie the pot to your back, not your front! It'll make climbing MUCH easier!'

Anansi almost fell out of the tree in surprise! 'Ouch!' he yelled, as he caught hold of a particularly big spike.

How ANNOYING that Ntikuma had spotted him! And how ANNOYING that his idea was such a good idea! After all, it was he, Anansi, who had the pot of wisdom!

Anansi threw the pot of wisdom down in a rage!

As the pot crashed to the ground, it shattered and tiny bits flew everywhere. And so did all the wisdom that was inside!

All the knowledge, all the skills and all the cleverness flew free and up, up, up into the air, floating away on the breeze!

As Anansi and Ntikuma watched,
storm clouds gathered above them.

Suddenly, there was a deafening clap
of thunder and it started to rain.

It rained ... and rained ... and rained. It rained so hard that the water washed the wisdom out of the air, onto the land and into the streams and rivers!

The rivers of wisdom flowed into the sea. And as the tides went in and out, around every bit of land, the wisdom began to spread around the whole, wide world.

'WOW!' was all that Anansi and Ntikuma could say, as they watched the amazing sight from the very highest, very driest place they could find.

So ... thanks to Anansi and his clever son, there is now a little bit of wisdom for everyone in the world.

And that includes you!

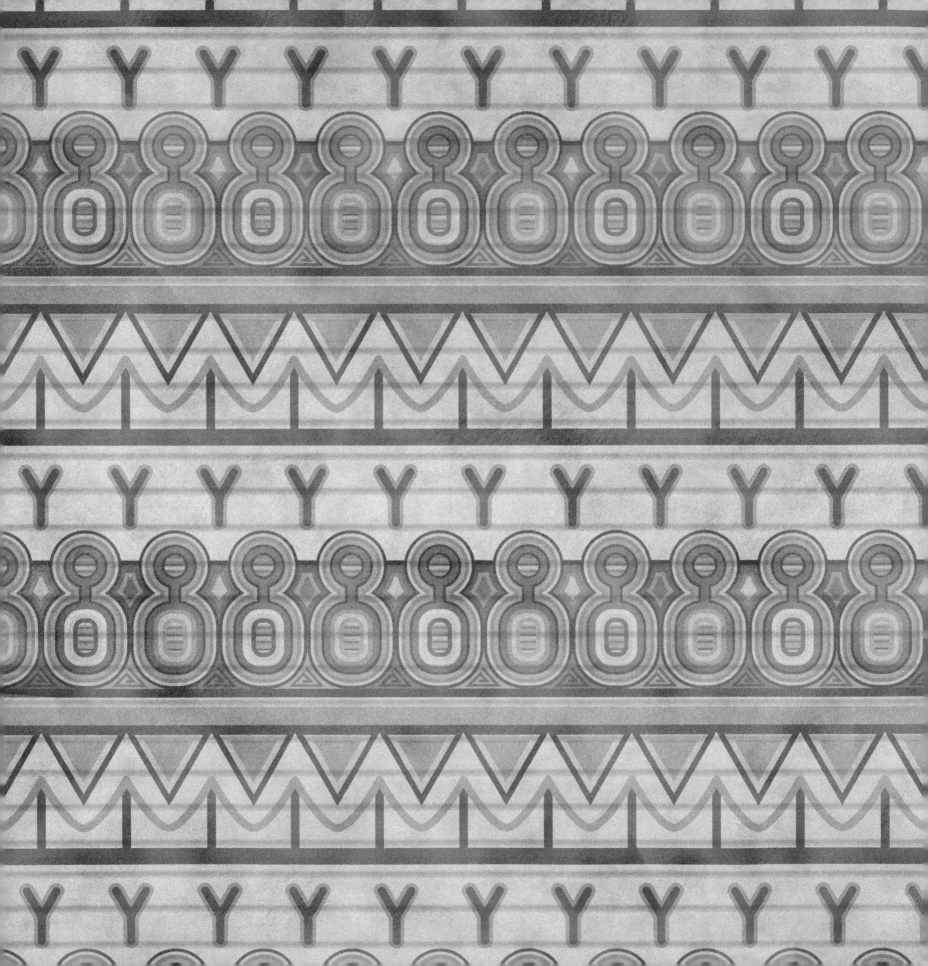